GIB MORGAN
OILMAN

by Ariane Dewey

GREENWILLOW BOOKS, New York

AUTHOR'S NOTE: Tales of the early oil fields are centered around Gib Morgan, Kemp Morgan, and Paul Bunyan. In contrast with Kemp Morgan and Paul Bunyan, Gib Morgan was a real oilman famous for his tall tales. In addition to the stories that Gib told about himself, I have included several incidents attributed to the imaginary characters. I have also made Gib the protagonist of anecdotes of the early oil industry.

—A. D.

REMEMBERING MY FATHER

The four-color preseparated illustrations combine black line art
and four half-tone overlays. The typeface is Bembo.

Library of Congress Cataloging-in-Publication Data

Dewey, Ariane.   Gib Morgan, oilman.
Summary: Retells the adventures of the
legendary oilman as he travels all over
the world drilling for oil.
[1. Morgan, Gib, 1842–1909.
2. Folklore—United States] I. Title.
PZ8.1.D54Gi   1987   398.2′2′0973   86-284
ISBN 0-688-06566-X   ISBN 0-688-06567-8 (lib. bdg.)

Gib Morgan was seventeen in 1859.
That year the first oil well was struck
at Titusville, Pennsylvania. It was near
where Gib lived.

Gib was smart and could fix anything, but he was tired of repairing wagon wheels, roofs, harnesses, and clocks. People were rushing to Oil Creek to make their fortunes. Gib bought himself some high-laced boots and a blue shirt and joined the crowd.

Derricks went up as thick as trees. The autumn rains soon turned the heavily traveled roads into deep rivers of mud. One day Gib kicked a hat floating by in the muddy street.

"Hey watch it!" shouted a voice. "That's my hat, and my head is in it."

"Quick, fellow, give me your hand so I can haul you out of this muck," offered Gib in alarm.

"No need, Stranger," said the man beneath the hat. "I've got a mule under me, and he's on solid ground."

His fame spread. If there was a problem,
Gib Morgan was the man to solve it.
The HARDLY EVER AND SCARCELY ABLE
GET OIL COMPANY sent Gib to see if there
was oil in the West Virginia hills.

Gib had never seen such steep slopes. The only piece of level ground big enough to hold his derrick was an old farmer's tiny corn patch. Gib built his rig while the old farmer continued hoeing.

At the end of each row, the farmer leaned on his hoe to rest.

SNAP CRACK . . . a puff of dust rose
from the edge of the field. The old fellow
had fallen right off his patch.
"Wait up," Gib hollered as he cast his
drilling cable over the edge of the field.

He caught the old man in mid air and
reeled him in like a fish.

"Guess you should have put up a fence,"
Gib said.

"It wasn't a fence I needed," replied the
old man. "It was a new hoe handle."

The WILDCAT WELLS UNLIMITED
COMPANY gave Gib a map of Colorado
with an X showing where to drill. When
Gib got there he discovered the cross
marked the tip top of Pike's Peak.
"Dang fool place for an oil well," Gib
announced. "But if that's what they
want, they've got it. There ain't no place
I can't drill." And he built his rig.

20

There was no room for the boiler and the steam engine on the peak so he put them in the valley. To drive the drill, he ran a huge belt, like a rubber band, that circulated from the engine to the mountaintop. Every morning Gib threw his saddle on the belt, yelled "GIDDY-UP," and rode up to work.

But just as he had thought, the Pike's
Peak well was a duster. It was dry!
"I knew it was a silly place to drill for oil,"
Gib muttered, and he headed for
California.

The well he drilled there came in with a
bang. It blew the rig apart and shot Gib
sky-high.

He was stuck high up there on top of a fountain of oil. A bird thought he was a tree and built a nest in his hair.

"I'd be mighty grateful if someone would get me off here," Gib shouted. It took three days to build a derrick tall enough to reach him.

The HARDLY EVER AND SCARCELY ABLE GET OIL COMPANY called Gib back to Pennsylvania. They needed a pipeline built from Oil Creek to the New Jersey coast. Gib knew that pipeliners have tremendous appetites.

"Buckwheat pancakes will fill them up," Gib decided. He had the batter mixed in a storage tank. From there it flowed through a pipeline and plopped onto huge griddles.

Each fifty-foot square griddle was heated by a gas well. Boys strapped sides of bacon to their feet and skated around to grease the pans. Girls flipped the pancakes with snow shovels. A conveyer belt delivered the pancakes to the one-half-mile-long counter. Each worker helped himself to at least thirty pancakes. They poured gallons of melted butter and hot syrup on top and devoured them. There was enough food for everyone.

By now Gib was supervising so many oil wells that he had to get around fast. A farmer in Kentucky had a horse that seemed just right. Gib traded a well for it. He called the horse Torpedo.

It was twenty-two yards long, weighed twenty tons, had three forward speeds, and could run in reverse.

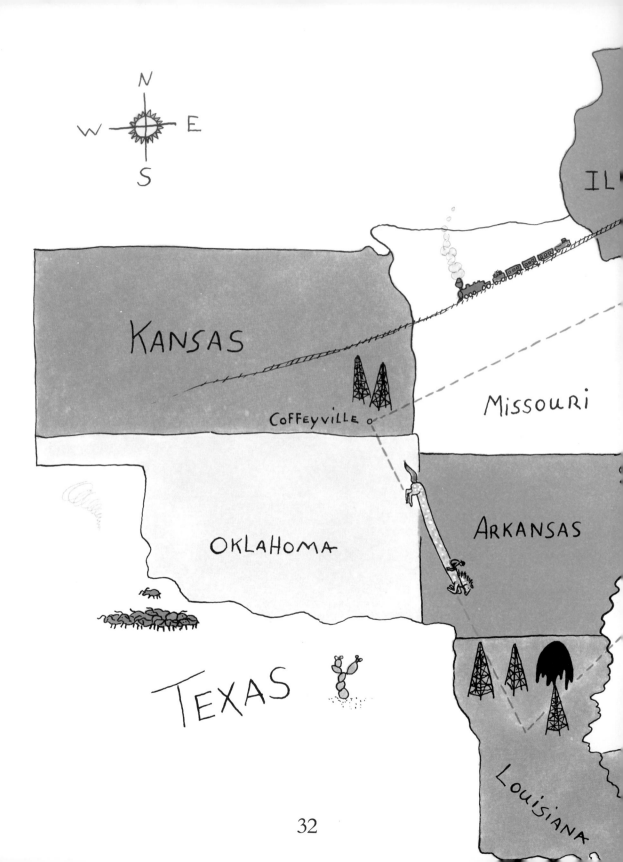

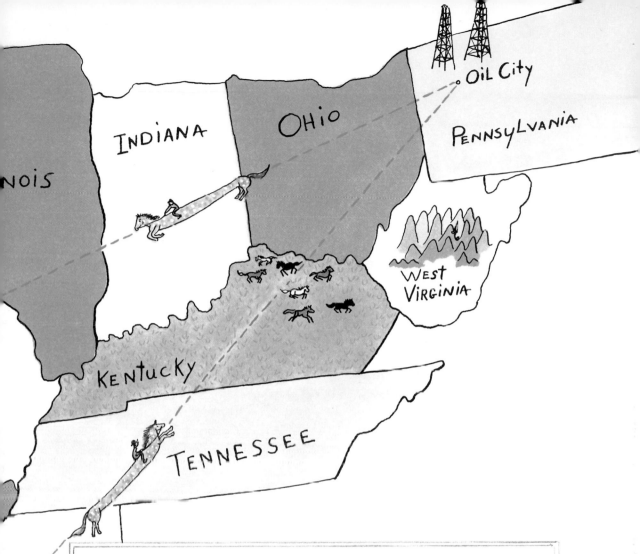

They could leave Oil City, Pennsylvania in the morning, get to Coffeyville, Kansas by noon, go to Louisiana in the afternoon, and still be back in Oil City in time for dinner. It sure beat taking the train.

They galloped down to Texas where
Gib built the biggest rig ever. It was so
high, the top part had hinges so that it
could fold back to let the moon go by.

36

It took fourteen days for a man to climb to the top to grease the pulley. Gib needed thirty men to work that rig. There were always fourteen men climbing up, fourteen coming down, one at the top working, and one resting at the bottom. Bunkhouses were spaced a day's climb apart so the men could eat and sleep. It was worth it because when that well blew in, it was the greatest gusher in the world.

The WE ALWAYS FIND OIL COMPANY sent Gib to South America next. The mosquitoes were terrible. Gib's crew lit a smoke fire for protection. It didn't work. Gib and his men hid in the thirty-thousand-barrel oil storage tank they were constructing.

Suddenly someone said, "Listen to those hailstones."

"That's not hail," drawled Gib. "That's skeeters."

Sure enough, those mosquitoes were diving against the tank in a fury. They drove their stingers right through the metal.

"Hammer them beaks over," shouted Gib. Soon the mosquitoes were pinned to the tank by their bent stingers.

It sounded like a hurricane as they
buzzed and beat their wings.
The tank had no floor as yet. The
mosquitoes lifted it right off the ground
and flew away with it. The men were
left standing there amazed.

Gib drilled and drilled. When he reached 10,000 feet he ran out of rope. But Gib knew there was oil down there. He could smell it. It would take two months to get more cable shipped in. Gib wandered into the jungle to think about what to do. And there was a boa constrictor sleeping off a meal. The boa was a mile long. Gib dragged him back to the well. The snake slept on.

43

Gib tied him to the end of the cable and continued drilling. It woke up the snake and he was mad! Gib served him a stack of flapjacks.

"I'll call you Strickie," Gib said. And that was the beginning of their friendship.

One day the drill bit came unfastened.
Strickic watched Gib try to fish it out of
the well. Suddenly he slithered down the
hole. When they pulled him up he had
the bit in his mouth.

The well went deeper and deeper and still no oil. Now they were running out of Strickie. They were so close everyone could smell oil. Strickie came to the rescue. He shed his skin. And that made the cable long enough to bring in a gusher.

By then Gib and his blue shirt were famous the world over. He'd drilled just about every kind of well there was, so he went back to the States and quit. He put his feet up and told tales of the oil fields. And no matter how tall they were, people believed him. OR ELSE. . . .